THE BO BEAR BOOKS

Bo Bear Learns to Share

Kamy Lynn Neumann
Illustrated by Brian S. Neumann

JACOB'S FUND

I met a beautiful woman who had an adorable but severely autistic son named Jacob. My heart immediately went out to this boy and his family. She told me that they had just got back from a trip to Panama City where he was able to receive one round of stem cell therapy and started showing encouraging signs of improvement. Although he can actually receive 3 or 4 treatments in total it is very expensive and she was hoping they could at least do one more. I knew I wanted to do something as I thought about my own precious boys. I remembered the Bo Bear Books and decided to use them as a means to create a fund for Jacob and other autistic children to receive beneficial treatments to help improve their condition. Half of the proceeds of every Bo Bear Book sold will go into Jacob's Fund. Thank you for your love and support of these beautiful children of God.

But Jacob replied, "I will not let you go unless you bless me." Genesis 32:26 NIV

The two little boys who inspired
The Bo Bear Books – Bo & Cody

Bo Bear has 5 cousins, two are girl cubs and three are boy cubs. They all live in cottages nearby and can get together often to explore caves and make forts and do everything cubs love to do.

CLUB
HOUSE

One of their most favorite things is to go fishing in the river and see who can catch the biggest fish. Bo Bear and his brother, Cody Cub, planned to meet the other boys by the river that afternoon.

"Last one to the other side is a rotten egg!" Bo Bear shouted at the other boys as he jumped in the river and began swimming to the other side.

Phoenix, Levi, Asher and Cody Cub all yelled as they jumped in after him. They swam half the day and fished the other half, filling their sacks they brought with them to collect their rich bounty.

"What a feast this will be!" Bo Bear exclaimed.

"Ya, won't the girls be jealous when they see all the fish WE will get to eat for dinner tonight?" Phoenix stated proudly.

"Mama, Mama, look at all our fish!"
Cody Cub cried out as they approached
the cottage and before the other cubs
could tell her first.

"My, my!" Mama B was quite impressed
as she looked in each sack.

“Where are the girls?” Asked Levi.

“In the kitchen,” replied Mama B, “filling jars with the honey from the honeycomb they found this afternoon.

"Honeycomb!" the boys cried in unison.
"What a treat! Guess they won't be
jealous after all!"

Miss Brooklyn and Miss Charlie had just
finished scooping the last bit of honey
into their little clay jars when the boys
came tumbling in with their sacks of fish.

"Do you have fresh fish from the river?"
Brooklyn asked.

"A whole bunch!" Bo Bear said. "If we
share our fish with you,
would you share your honeycomb with
us?"

"Of course!" The girls responded.
"Everyone knows there's nothing better
than honey smoked fish!"

That night everyone feasted on the most
mouth watering, honey-dripping, smoked
fish they had ever eaten in all the Woods.
And Bo Bear realized that it pays to
share with others...even girls!

Give, and it will be given to you. A good measure, pressed down, shaken together and running over, will be poured into your lap...Luke 6:38 NIV

THE BO BEAR BOOKS
Collection:

Bo Bear Plays Drums

Bo Bear Meets Cody Cub

Bo Bear Learns to Help

Bo Bear Learns to Share

Bo Bear Gets Stuck

Available now at <u>amazon.com</u>

9 781636 250670